GREYLING

GREYLING

JANE YOLEN

ILLUSTRATED BY DAVID RAY

PHILOMEL BOOKS

NEW YORK

Text copyright © 1968 and 1991 by Jane Yolen.
Illustrations copyright © 1991 by David Ray.
Published by Philomel Books, a division of
The Putnam & Grosset Group, 200 Madison Avenue,
New York, NY 10016. Published simultaneously in Canada.
All rights reserved. Original edition published in 1968 by
The World Publishing Company, Cleveland, Ohio.
Printed in Hong Kong by South China Printing Co. (1988) Ltd.
Book design by Gunta Alexander.

Library of Congress Cataloging-in-Publication Data
Yolen, Jane.
Greyling / by Jane Yolen; illustrated by David Ray.
p.   cm.   Summary: A selchie, a seal transformed into human
form, lives on land with a lonely fisherman and his wife, until
the day a great storm threatens the fisherman's life.
ISBN 0-399-22262-6
[1. Seals (Animals) — Fiction.]   I. Ray, David, 1940-   ill. II. Title.
PZ7.Y78Gq 1991 [E] — dc20 90-35395 CIP AC

48136

For David with love and singing.
—J.Y.

To my father, Angus, and to Wayne.
—D.R.

Once on a time when wishes were aplenty, a fisherman and his wife lived by the side of the sea. All that they ate came out of the sea.

Their hut was covered with the finest mosses that kept them cool in the summer and warm in the winter. And there was nothing they needed or wanted except a child.

Each morning, when the moon touched down behind the water and the sun rose up behind the plains, the wife would say to the fisherman, "You have your boat and your nets and your lines. But I have no baby to hold in my arms." And again in the evening it was the same. She would weep and wail and rock the cradle that stood by the hearth. But year in and year out the cradle stayed empty.

Now the fisherman was also sad that they had no child. But he kept his sorrow to himself so that his wife would not know his grief and thus double her own.

Indeed, he would leave the hut each morning with a breath of song and return each night with a whistle on his lips. His nets were full but his heart was empty, yet he never told his wife.

One sunny day, when the beach was a tan thread spun between the sea and plain, the fisherman as usual went down to his boat. But this day he found a small grey seal stranded on the sandbar, crying for its own.

The fisherman looked up the beach and down. He looked in front of him and behind. And he looked to the town on the great grey cliffs that sheared off into the sea. But there were no other seals in sight.

So he shrugged his shoulders and took off his shirt. Then he dipped it into the water and wrapped the seal pup carefully in its folds.

"You have no father and you have no mother," he said. "And I have no child. So you shall come home with me."

And the fisherman did no fishing that day but brought the seal pup, wrapped in his shirt, straight home to his wife.

When she saw him coming home early with no shirt on, the fisherman's wife ran out of the hut, fear riding in her heart. Then she looked wonderingly at the bundle that he held in his arms.

"It is nothing," he said, "but a seal pup I found stranded in the shallows and longing for its own. I thought we could give it love and care until it is old enough to seek its kin."

The fisherman's wife nodded and took the bundle. Then she uncovered the wrapping and gave a loud cry. "Nothing!" she said. "You call this nothing?"

The fisherman looked. Instead of a seal lying in the folds, there was a strange child with great grey eyes and silvery grey hair, smiling up at him.

The fisherman wrung his hands. "It is a selchie," he cried. "I have heard of them. They are men upon the land and seals in the sea. I thought it was but a tale."

"Then he shall remain a man upon the land," said the fisherman's wife, clasping the child in her arms, "for I shall never let him return to the sea."

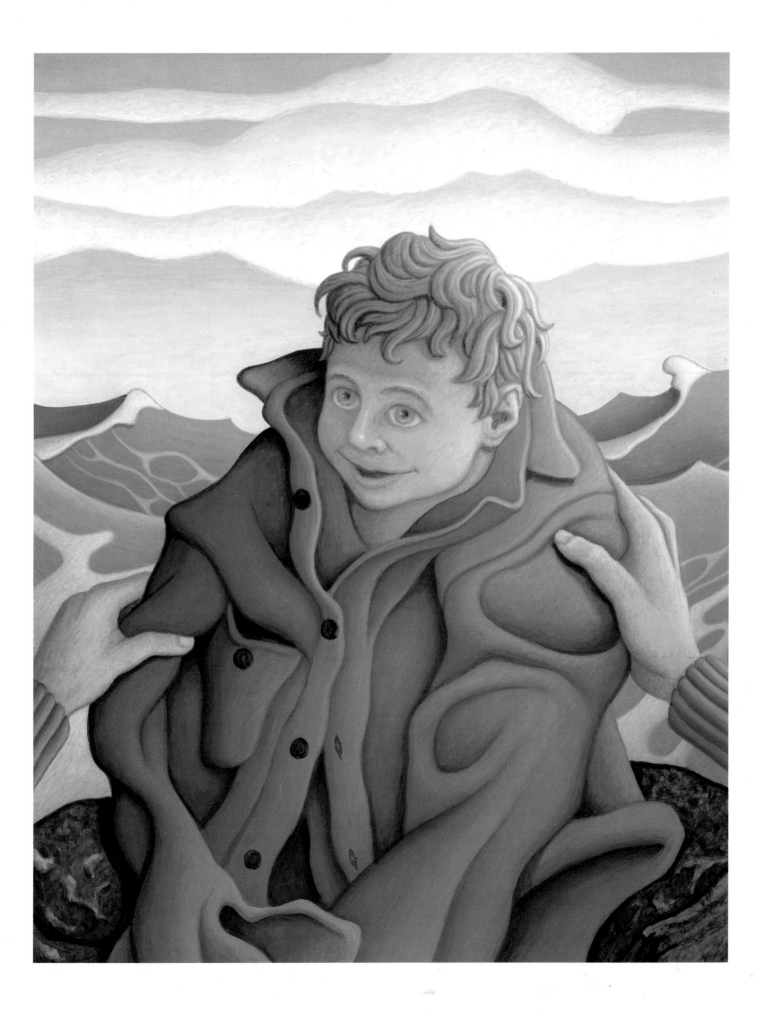

"Never," agreed the fisherman, for he knew how his wife had wanted a child. And in his secret heart, he wanted one too. Yet he felt somehow it was wrong.

"We shall call him Greyling," said the fisherman's wife, "for his eyes and hair are the color of a storm-coming sky. Greyling, though he has brought sunlight into our home."

And though they still lived by the side of the water in a hut covered with mosses that kept them warm in the winter and cool in the summer, the boy Greyling was never allowed in the sea.

He grew from a child to a lad. He grew from a lad to a young man. He gathered driftwood for his mother's hearth and searched the tide pools for shells for her mantel. He mended his father's nets and tended his father's boat. But though he often stood by the shore or high in the town on the great grey cliffs, looking and longing and grieving his heart for what he did not really know, he never went into the sea.

Then one wind-wailing morning, just fifteen years from the day that Greyling had been found, a great storm blew up suddenly in the North. It was such a storm as had never been seen before; the sky turned nearly black and even the fish had trouble swimming. The wind pushed huge waves onto the shore. The waters gobbled up the little hut on the beach. And Greyling and the fisherman's wife were forced to flee to the town high on the great grey cliffs. There they looked down at the roiling, boiling sea.

Far from shore they spied the fisherman's boat, its sails flapping like the wings of a wounded gull. And clinging to the broken mast was the fisherman himself, sinking deeper with every wave.

The fisherman's wife gave a terrible cry. "Will no one save him?" she called to the people of the town who had gathered on the edge of the cliff. "Will no one save my own dear husband, who is all of life to me?"

But the townsmen looked away. There was no man there who dared risk his life in that sea, even to save a drowning soul.

"Will no one at all save him?" she cried out again.

"Let the boy go," said one old man, pointing at Greyling with his stick. "He looks strong enough."

But the fisherman's wife clasped Greyling in her arms and held his ears with her hands. She did not want him to go into the sea. She was afraid he would never return.

"Will no one save my own dear heart?" cried the fisherman's wife for a third and last time.

But shaking their heads, the people of the town edged to their houses and shut their doors and locked their windows and set their backs to the ocean and their faces to the fires that glowed in every hearth.

"I will save him, Mother," cried Greyling, "or die as I try."

And before she could tell him no, he broke from her grasp and dived from the top of the great cliffs, down, down, down into the tumbling sea.

"He will surely sink," whispered the women as they ran from their warm fires to watch.

"He will certainly drown," called the men as they took down their spyglasses from the shelves.

They gathered on the cliffs and watched the boy dive down into the sea.

As Greyling disappeared beneath the waves, little fingers of foam tore at his clothes. They snatched his shirt and his pants and his shoes and sent them bubbling away to the shore.

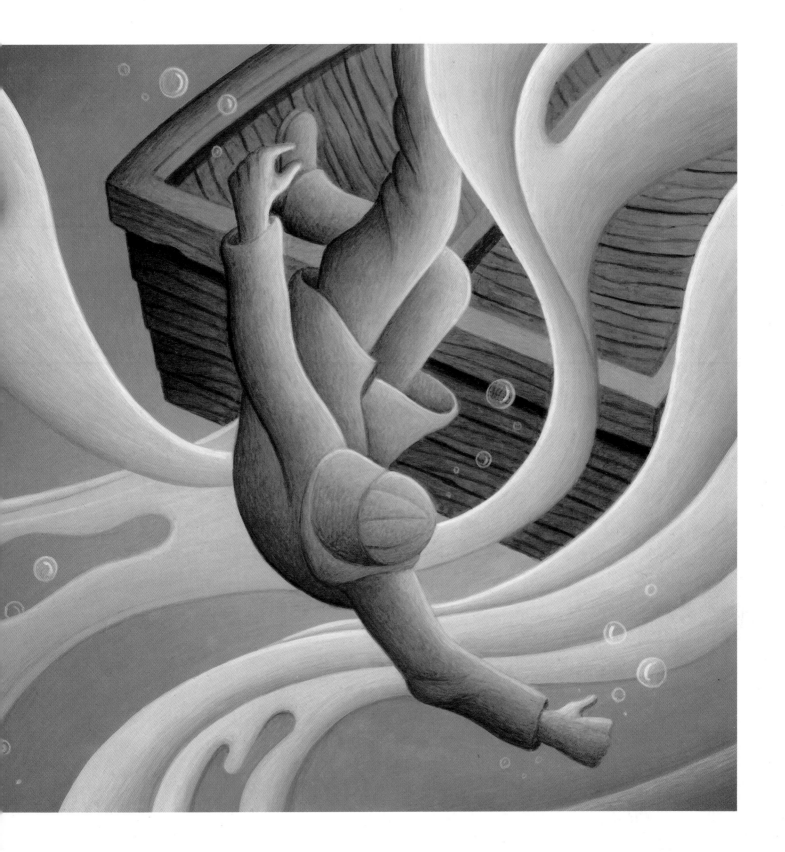

And as Greyling went deeper beneath the waves, even his skin seemed to slough off till he swam, free at last, in the sleek grey coat of a great grey seal.

The selchie had returned to the sea.

But the people of the town did not see this. All they saw was the diving boy disappearing under the waves and then, farther out, a large seal swimming toward the boat that wallowed in the sea. The sleek grey seal, with no effort at all, eased the fisherman to the shore though the waves were wild and bright with foam. And then, with a final salute, it turned its back on the land and headed joyously out to sea.

The fisherman's wife hurried down to the sand. And behind her followed the people of the town. They searched up the beach and down, but they did not find the boy.

"A brave son," said the men when they found his shirt, for they thought he was certainly drowned.

"A very brave son," said the women when they found his shoes, for they thought him lost for sure.

"Has he really gone?" asked the fisherman's wife of her husband when at last they were alone.

"Yes, quite gone," the fisherman said to her. "Gone where his heart calls, gone to the great wide sea. And though my heart grieves at his leaving, it tells me this way is best."

The fisherman's wife sighed. And then she cried. But at last she agreed that perhaps it was best. "For he is both man and seal," she said. "And though we cared for him for a while, now he must care for himself." And she never cried again.

So once more they lived alone by the side of the sea in a new little hut that was covered with mosses to keep them warm in the winter and cool in the summer.

Yet once a year a great grey seal is seen at night near the fisherman's home. And the people in town talk of it, and wonder. But seals do come to the shore and men do go to the sea; and so the townfolk do not dwell upon it very long.

But it is no ordinary seal. It is Greyling himself come home
— come to tell his parents tales of the lands that lie far beyond
the waters, and to sing them songs of the wonders that lie far
beneath the sea.

A Note About the Seal Legends

The fisherfolk who live in the Scottish islands of Shetland and Orkney, and as far west as the Hebrides, tell many strange and beautiful tales of the *selchies*, the seals who take on human form. Among their traditional folk songs is *The Great Selchie of Sule Skerrie*; the lovely pentatonic melody and the traditional words are of very ancient origin.

I am a man up - on the land. I am a Sel - chie_ on the sea. And when I'm far frae eve - ry strand My_ dwell - ing is in Sule Sker - rie.